THE NUNG GUAMA

Roger Lancelyn Green

BBC/LONGMAN

A poor widow-woman was walking along the road, taking a present of cakes to her parents, when a Nung-Guama sprang out of a clump of bamboo just in front of her.

"Heuch! Heuch!" cried the Nung-Guama,
and the widow fell on her knees, all of a tremble.
It's better to be eaten by a tiger, or a dragon,
or even a snake than by a Nung-Guama:
for Nung-Guamas are messy eaters. Of all things,
they most enjoy human flesh.

"Give me those delicious cakes!"
golloped the Nung-Guama.

"I can't do that," sobbed the widow,
"they are for my parents."

"Then I'll eat you instead," gurgled
the Nung-Guama. "I'll come to your house tonight,
and pull you to pieces with my claws, and
chew you up with my big teeth. Heuch! Heuch!"

The widow screamed and hid her face. When she looked up, the Nung-Guama had gone. But still she crouched on the ground.

Presently a pedlar came plodding by with his pack on his back.
"Honourable Lady," he said,
"why are you shrieking and sobbing?"

"I've seen a Nung-Guama," she moaned,
"and he's coming tonight
to tear me in pieces and eat me."

"Are you sure it was a Nung-Guama?" asked the pedlar. "Tell me what he was like."

"He was indeed a Nung-Guama," sobbed the widow. "His body was like a bull, and his head was as big as a wine-jar. His feet were big and soft and floppy, I could hear them going flap-flosh as he walked. And he had dirty hair and horrid hands with big, sharp claws."

"Certainly that was a Nung-Guama, and Nung-Guamas are messy eaters," said the pedlar. "I can do nothing for you. But here's a present of a packet of needles. You can stick them in the door of your house, and perhaps they'll prick the Nung-Guama."

Then the pedlar shouldered his pack,
and went on his way.
But the widow went on lying by the roadside.

Presently a farmer came by with
a load of manure to spread on his fields.
"Honourable Lady," he said,
"why are you shrieking and sobbing?"

"I've seen a Nung-Guama," she moaned,
"and he's coming tonight
to tear me in pieces and eat me."

The farmer said: “I can do nothing for you, but here’s a present of some of my manure. Spread it on your door, and perhaps when the Nung-Guama finds that he’s got his hands dirty, he may go away.”

Then the farmer went on his way to the field. But the widow went on lying by the roadside.

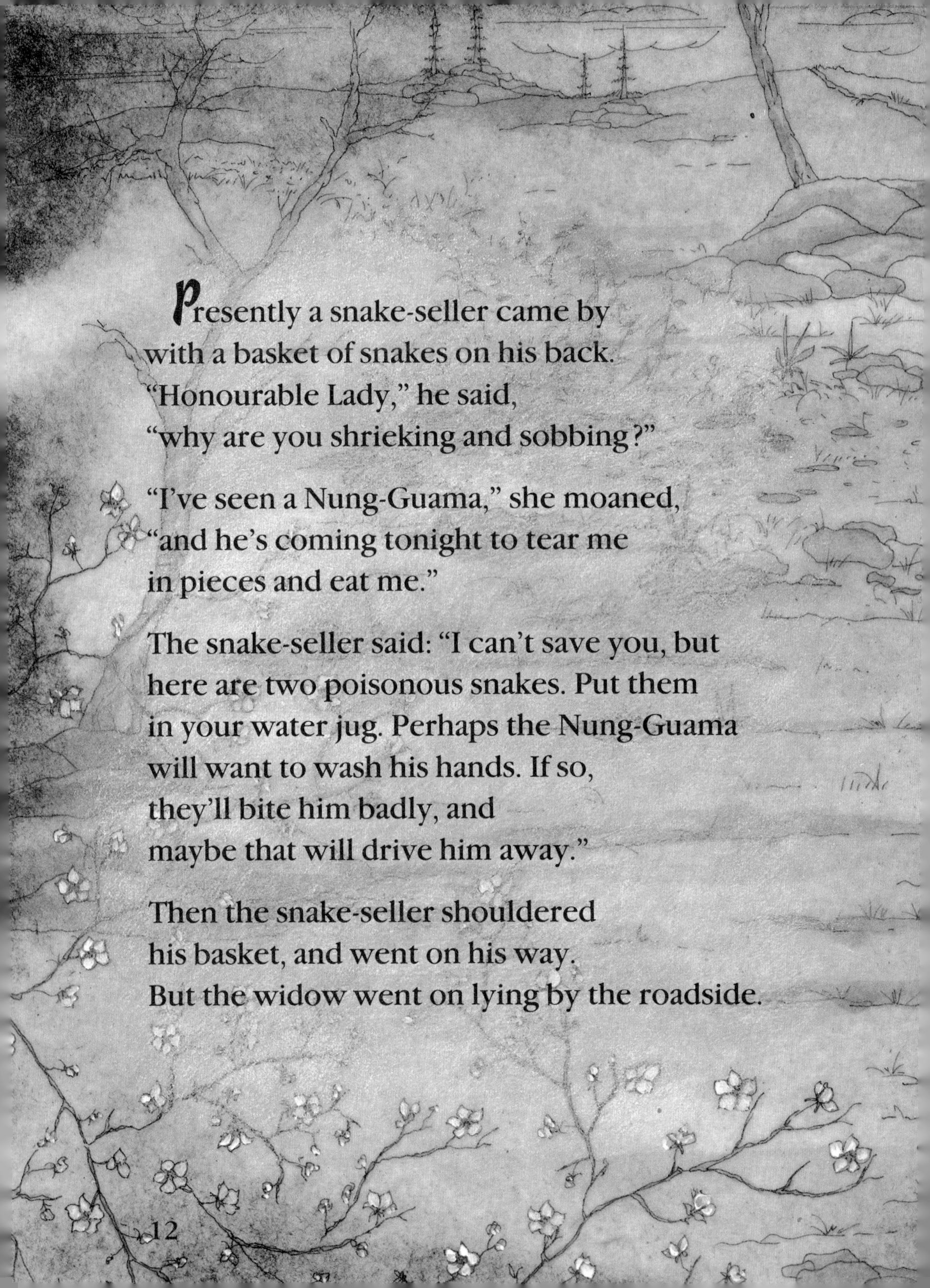

Presently a snake-seller came by
with a basket of snakes on his back.
"Honourable Lady," he said,
"why are you shrieking and sobbing?"

"I've seen a Nung-Guama," she moaned,
"and he's coming tonight to tear me
in pieces and eat me."

The snake-seller said: "I can't save you, but
here are two poisonous snakes. Put them
in your water jug. Perhaps the Nung-Guama
will want to wash his hands. If so,
they'll bite him badly, and
maybe that will drive him away."

Then the snake-seller shouldered
his basket, and went on his way.
But the widow went on lying by the roadside.

Presently a fishmonger came by,
carrying a basket full of fishes.
"Honourable Lady," he said,
"why do you lie there moaning and sobbing?"

"I've seen a Nung-Guama," she cried,
"and he's coming tonight to tear me
in pieces and eat me."

The fishmonger said: "I can't protect you, but take these two flat fishes. Don't boil them, or they'll be useless, but keep them in the pot. When he's been bitten by the snakes, the Nung-Guama may want to bathe his wounds in the warm water of the cooking pot. Then these fishes may fasten their teeth in him and he may be so fed up that he'll run home."

Then the fishmonger slung his basket over his shoulder and went on his way. But the widow went on lying by the roadside.

Presently an egg-seller came along, crying,
"Hundred-year-old eggs for sale!"
"Honourable Lady," he said,
"why are you snivelling and sobbing?"

"I've seen a Nung-Guama," she gasped,
"and he's coming tonight
to pull me to pieces and eat me."

The egg-seller said: "I can't rescue you,
but take this present of eggs, and place them
in the warm ashes on your hearth.
When the Nung-Guama has been bitten by the
fishes and the snakes, his fingers will bleed.

The best cure for that is to plunge them
in warm, flaky ashes. If he does that,
the hundred-year-old eggs will burst
in his face, and their disgusting stink
will drive him away."

Then the egg-seller raised the rest of his eggs
with great care, and went on his way.

Presently a supplier of millstones turned up,
staggering under a huge heavy stone
shaped like a wheel.
"Honourable Lady," he said,
"how comes it that you crouch here
too exhausted to shed a single tear?"

"I've seen a Nung-Guama," she replied
in a hoarse whisper, "and he's returning
after dark to claw me in pieces
and gobble me up."

The supplier of millstones said:
"I'm not able to help you, but accept this gift
of a Guaranteed First Class Ace Positively A.1
Millstone of colossal weight! Hang it
from the ceiling near your bed. As soon as
the Nung-Guama is underneath it, cut the rope
that holds it up, and let it land
on the creature's head with colossal force.
Here's an iron bar to finish him off."

Then the supplier of millstones turned home
for another millstone.

Evening had come. The widow collected up her gifts. She was so upset that she ate all her cakes, quite forgetting her duty to her parents.

Then she hired several porters, and set off for home.

She was quite certain that she would be eaten by the Nung-Guama, but nevertheless she did with all her presents exactly as she had been advised to do.

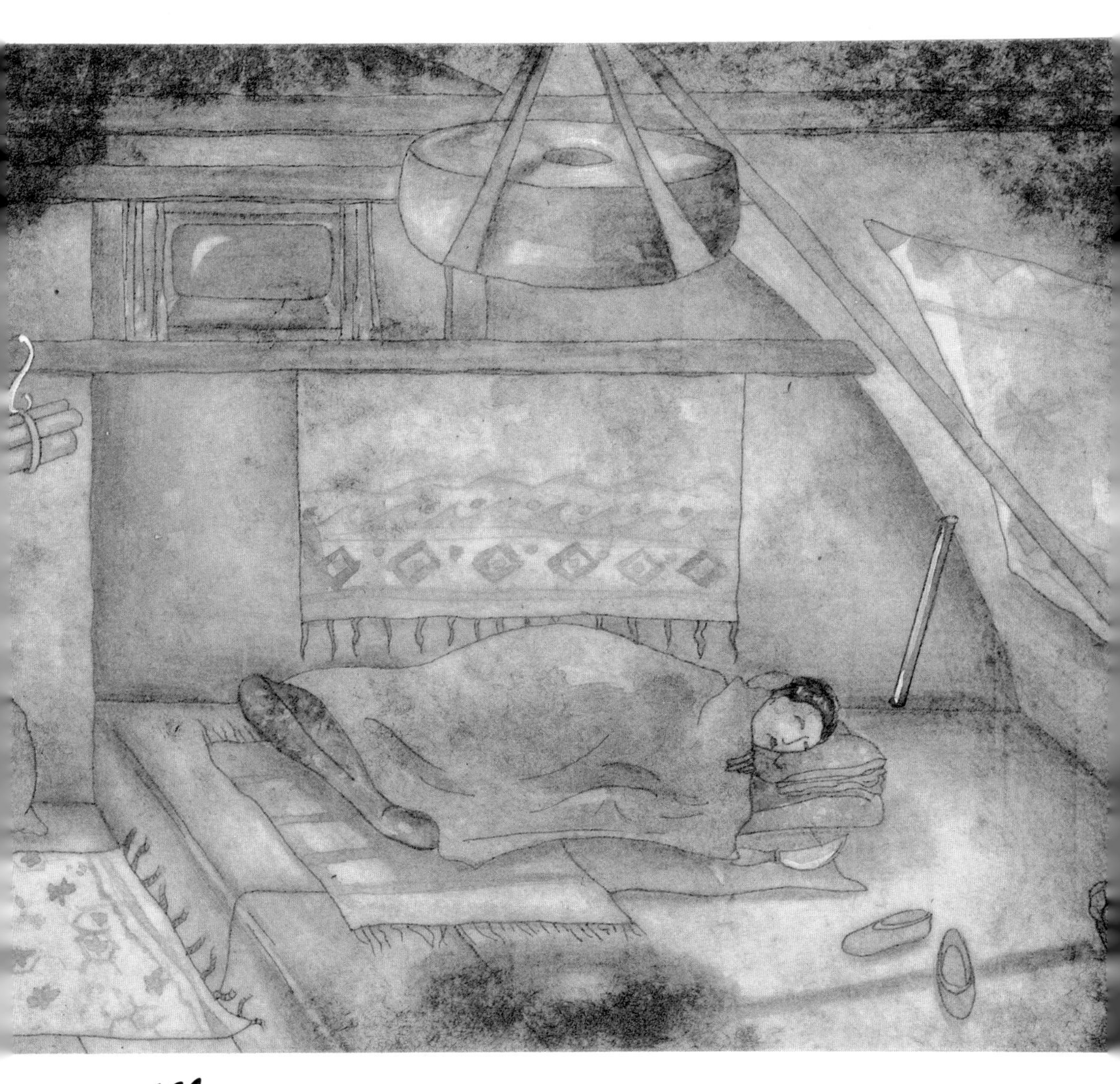

When this was done, it was quite dark.
So she got undressed and went to bed.

All of a sudden, in the middle of the night,
she woke up with a start to hear a sound
of "Flap-Flosh! Flap-Flosh! Flap-Flosh!"
drawing nearer and nearer. Then she heard
a horrible "Heuch! Heuch!"
and the voice of the Nung-Guama gurgling:
"Open the door, you nice plump widow-woman!
I want to munch you and scrunch you
and guzzle you up!"
"Let yourself in, Honourable Nung-Guama,"
answered the widow, "for I am in bed."

With a roar of rage the Nung-Guama beat down the door; and then he howled in his horrible squelchy voice as the needles tore him and the muck dirtied him:
"Ah, how prickly and filthy! But I'll mash her!

Good, here's water to wash my hands . . .

Ouch! Ouch!
I'm bitten by snakes! What a hideous hovel this is!

Ah, the very thing: warm water to bathe
my wounds . . .

Och! Och!
I'm bitten by sharks! I'm bleeding to death!

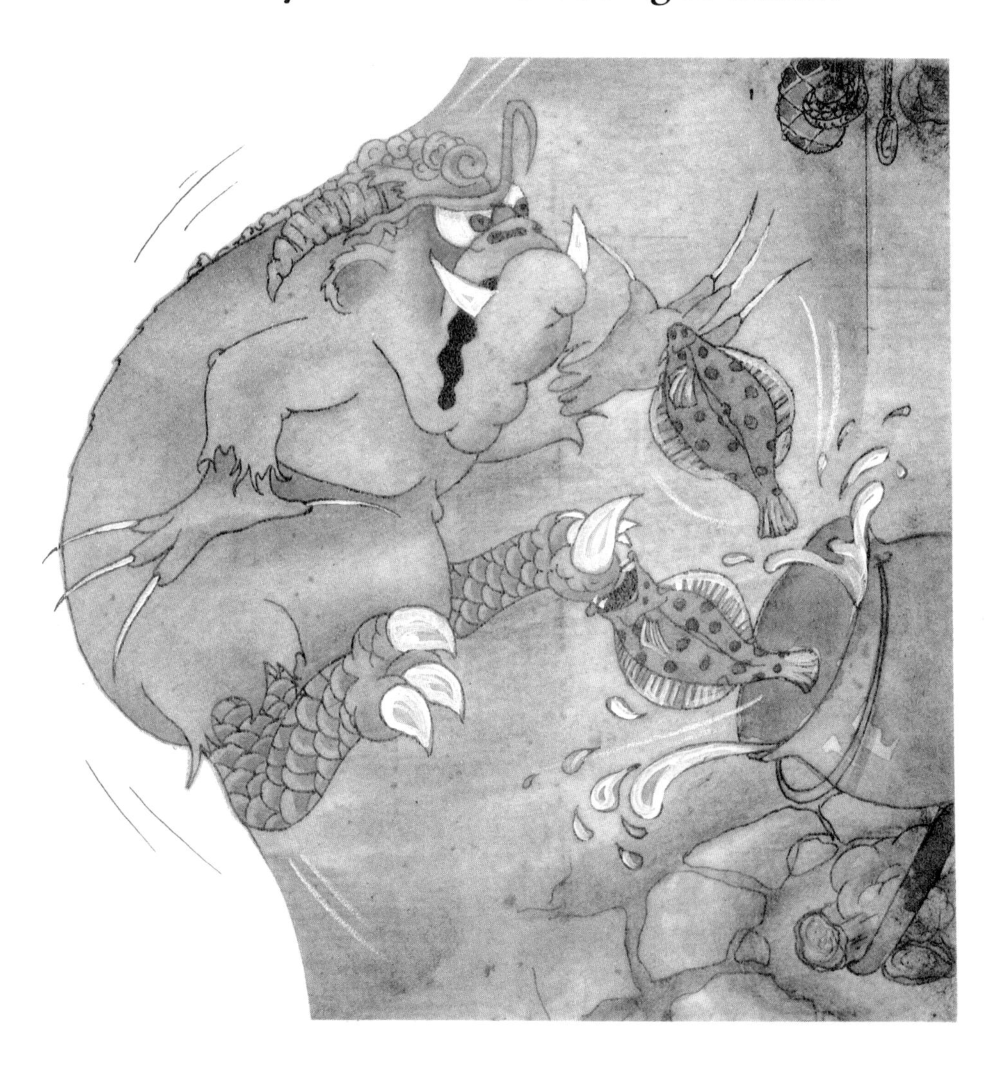

Good! Warm ashes to stop the blood . . .
Euch! Euch!
Bad bombs bursting in my eyes!
Oh, I'll chew and chaw and chomp
this nasty widow-woman!
Where are you, hideous hag?"

And he came "Flap-Flosh! Flap-Flosh!" across the floor.

When he was under the millstone, the widow cut the string. The millstone crushed the Nung-Guama's head as if it had been a hundred-year-old egg. But she got out and gave the rest of him a few good strokes with the iron bar, just to make sure.

Then she got back into bed and went to sleep.

Next day she found her house in a terrible mess. But she skinned the Nung-Guama, and sold his skeleton so well that it paid all her bills, and left her a nice little sum over for herself. And the Nung-Guama's hide kept her warm in bed for the rest of her life.

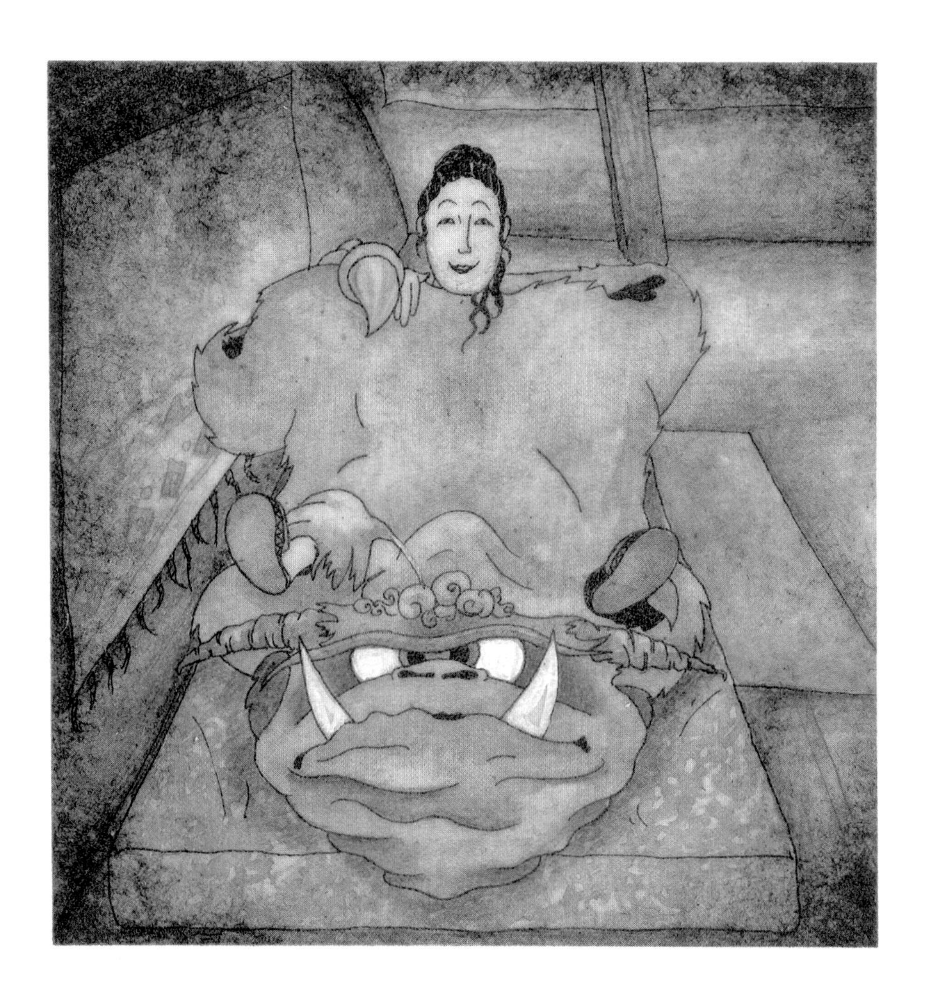

Other titles in this series

The reindeer herder and the moon by Bob Barton
The tiger and the poor man by Beulah Candappa
The green man by Gail Haley
Who's afraid now? by Rose Impey
The days of the banyan tree by Madhur Jaffrey
Miss MacDonald had a zoo by Cecily O'Neill
In the middle of the night by Philippa Pearce
Open wide by Mary Rayner
The nagging husband by James Riordan

Series consultants: Myra Barrs and Sue Ellis, Director and Deputy Director of the Centre for Learning in Primary Education (Southwark).

The series accompanies the BBC School Radio series, *Listening and Reading* on Radio 5 Medium Wave.

Published by BBC Educational Publishing and Longman Group UK Limited

BBC Educational Publishing
a division of
BBC Enterprises Limited
Woodlands
80 Wood Lane
London W12 0TT

Longman Group Limited
Longman House
Burnt Mill
Harlow
Essex CM20 2JE
England and associated
companies throughout the world

First published in Great Britain in 1962 in 'Once Long Ago, Tales of the World' by Golden Pleasure Books Limited

Series editor Joan Griffiths
Cover and book design by
Rob Green
(school edition) ISBN 0 582 06206 3
(trade edition) ISBN 0 563 34761 9

Set in 16/20pt Garamond book ITC
Typeset by Goodfellow and Egan
Text and cover origination by
Dot Gradations
Printed and bound by Cambus Litho